Dragon + fly

Car + wash

Key + hole

Rain + bow

Toad + Stool

Bee + hive

Book + Store

THE COMPOUND NOUN
TREASURE
HUNT

KIMBERLEE GARD

illustrations by
SANDIE SONKE

To children everywhere:
May you always find what
your heart is looking for.
—K.G.

For Cole and Annabel.
—S.S.

Text copyright © 2025 by Kimberlee Gard
Illustration copyright © 2025 by Sandie Sonke
All rights reserved.

Published by Familius LLC, www.familius.com
PO Box 1130, Sanger, CA 93657

Familius books are available at special discounts for bulk purchases, whether for sales promotions or for family or corporate use. For more information, contact Familius Sales at orders@familius.com.

Reproduction of this book in any manner, in whole or in part, without written permission of the publisher is prohibited.

Library of Congress Control Number: 2025933191

Print ISBN 9781641708852
Ebook ISBN 9798893960716

Printed in China

Edited by Brooke Jorden and Leah Welker
Cover and book design by Brooke Jorden

10 9 8 7 6 5 4 3 2 1

First Edition

THE COMPOUND NOUN
TREASURE HUNT

KIMBERLEE GARD

illustrations by
SANDIE SONKE

It all started when a BULL...

...DOG stumbled upon a piece of paper.

"It must be a treasure map," Bulldog said. "And it must lead to gold!"

The hunt was on until DRAGON...

. . . FLY stopped him.

"What are you doing?" she asked.

"Looking for gold."

Dragonfly pointed to a SUN...

...FLOWER. "That looks like gold."

"No," said Bulldog. "It's not the gold I'm looking for."

Something buzzed past them. "Look, a BEE..."

"...HIVE! Honey looks like gold."

"No," said Bulldog. "It's not the gold I'm looking for."

They peeked under a spotted TOAD...

...STOOL.

"No gold there," Dragonfly said.
"Maybe around the HEDGE . . .

...HOG."

"Still no gold," said Bulldog.

They chased after a rolling WHEEL...

...BARROW.

"Could this be it?" Dragonfly asked.

"No," said Bulldog. "It's not the gold I'm looking for."

The sky turned cloudy,
then came the RAIN...

... BOW.

"Maybe there's a pot of gold at the end!"

But there wasn't any.

They looked behind the BALL...

...PARK.

But still no gold.

"Maybe we could find a clue in the BOOK...

...STORE."

There were lots of books but no clues and no gold.

Beep! Beep! went a horn, and they jumped into a CAR...

...WASH.

Absolutely no gold in a carwash!

That's when they saw a FOOT...

... PRINT.

The footprint led to another.

"Let's follow them!"

They hurried to a door with a **KEY**...

...HOLE. "The gold must be inside!"

They peeked through the keyhole.

And there it was, one GOLD...

Hedge + hog

Sun + flower

Wheel + barrow

Ball + park

Gold + fish

Bull + dog

Foot + print